HOW TO EAT A PEACH

By Karen Schaufeld

Illustrations by Kurt Schwarz

Quidne Press
Smart Books for Smart Kids

Published by Quidne Press

Quidne Press
Smart Books for Smart Kids

Library of Congress Control Number: TXu002123248

Illustrated by Kurt Schwarz

Quidne Press

www.Quidnepress.org

Hardcover:

ISBN - 978-0-9972299-2-9

Author photo by Renss Greene/Loudoun Now

To Max, Jake, and Haley,
who have followed their passions.

Tree stood proudly against the blue sky, overlooking the other peach trees and protected by a wall.

Farmer Fred patrolled the wall with his rifle to make sure no other person or creature would steal the peaches from Tree. He had no wife and no children, so Tree was his family. Tasting a peach just plucked off the branch was as close to eating heaven as you could get.

Sadly, no one but Farmer Fred or the judges at the county fair ever got to taste these perfect peaches. What wasn't picked and eaten was left to rot on the ground.

Squirrel was born to love peaches.
Their sweet aroma mingled with his
first breath. He barely tolerated nuts
and seeds. From the moment his
squirrel teeth burst through the warm,
fuzzy skin, he dreamed only of peaches.

Squirrel was different. He didn't chase
other squirrels or play "dodge the car." He
climbed trees only to sample a peach from
each tree in the orchard. Squirrel knew he
was meant to be a connoisseur of peaches.

Squirrel's mother thought his peach
obsession was a little weird, but she saw
how strong he was getting climbing trees.
At night, when she gently stroked his sleepy
head, she let him know that his passion will
lead him where he was meant to go.

One day, Squirrel saw Tree alone
on its hill surrounded by the wall.
Its fruits were still young, small and
green, clinging tightly to its branches.
The wall was smooth, tall and spiky,
designed so that no creature, especially
squirrels, could ever get a pawhold on it.
Squirrel knew that this peach tree must
be special to be so protected, which
meant that Squirrel had to eat a peach
from Tree.

As the peaches in the orchard ripened, Squirrel methodically noted the unique taste, texture, color and juiciness from each tree. He also noted when Farmer Fred took a break from guard duty protecting Tree.

Strengthened from eating peaches, Squirrel tried to climb over, dig under or catapult onto the wall, but again and again, he fell short.

Squirrel slid tired and disheartened
onto his back. . . and that's when Farmer
Fred gave him an idea. Squirrel didn't
have big pieces of wood, but he had
small twigs. Squirrel didn't have a
hammer and nails, but he had grassy
twine and strong teeth. And Squirrel
had determination.

It was late summer, and Tree's peaches would ripen and fall off soon, so Squirrel worked day and night to gather and gnaw twigs into just the right shape.

His little paws ached as he wrapped the dried grasses around each joint to hold the steps and rails tightly together. The other squirrels laughed at Squirrel's labors. They thought he was nuts.

On the day he finished his squirrel ladder, Squirrel waited for Farmer Fred to take his break before dragging it to the base of the wall. He knew life would never be the same as he swung his legs over the top and fell onto the grass on the other side.

Tree's leaves were a deep lush green. Its wood was a rich, dark brown, and its peaches were a harmonious blend of pink, orange and yellow. The smell of ripened peaches was so alluring that Squirrel was drawn up Tree's trunk to grasp a peach.

He scrambled to the ground, totally
focused on eating the peach. As he bit
into it, his eyes grew round and moist.
Yes! This peach was everything Squirrel
had dreamed of and hoped for his whole
life. As the juices from the peach ran
down his jowls, its rich sweet taste
filling his mouth, he had tears of joy
that all his hard work was worth it. He
closed his eyes to savor the moment.

The trance ended abruptly when he opened his eyes and was staring into the barrel of Farmer Fred's gun. Squirrel looked for an escape, but he had only thought of getting in, not getting out. Squirrel was frozen in fear as his triumph was about to become a tragedy.

Farmer Fred paused. He couldn't pull
the trigger. A squirrel so determined
that he built a ladder may just realize
how special Tree's peaches are.

Squirrel saw Farmer Fred's eyes soften as he sat down next to the petrified squirrel.

"I need help," Farmer Fred began, "It has been my lonely life's work to guard my perfect peaches for so many years."

Farmer Fred picked up Squirrel's half-eaten fruit and handed it back to him. "If you help me keep thieves away, I will share the peaches with you."

And so their mutual vigilance began.
Farmer Fred marched around beneath
Tree every day, and Squirrel marched
around behind him carrying a little
wooden rifle that Farmer Fred had
carved for him.

Squirrel missed his mom, but he knew
he had a job and a purpose.

Farmer Fred strung two hammocks in Tree's branches. At night, Farmer Fred told Squirrel stories of how he pruned and nurtured Tree when it was young.

The hammocks gently swayed in the summer breeze and as fireflies illuminated the branches above them, Farmer Fred told Squirrel, "Now, Tree is your life's work too."

Tree's leaves turned orange and fell off in the autumn wind, and even though there were no more peaches to steal when the winter cold came, Squirrel built a lookout nest which he lined with dried grasses. Farmer Fred brought Squirrel acorns to survive the winter.

Sometimes Farmer Fred would build a little fire and Squirrel would curl up inside Farmer Fred's coat as he talked about their plans for next spring.

When spring came, Farmer Fred and Squirrel fell into a predictable rhythm of caring for Tree. Squirrel picked off bugs as Farmer Fred delicately trimmed the branches. They patrolled together during the day and swung in their hammocks at night. When spring turned to summer, together they watched in wonder as the peaches grew fragrant and colorful.

One bright summer day, the sun was briefly blocked when Girl Squirrel sailed over the wall, clasping a tattered scrap of blanket, emblazoned with red hearts, in her tiny paws. She landed on a branch and fulfilled her lifelong dream; to eat the perfect peach.

As Girl Squirrel was savoring her first bite of the sweet, fuzzy peach, she was confronted by Squirrel, who couldn't fire his carved wooden rifle, but was prepared to beat any intruder with it.

Girl Squirrel's eyes widened with fear, and she dropped her stolen fruit. Her joy had turned to horror.

Squirrel was in a difficult position.

Squirrel realized he could not fault Girl Squirrel for their shared passion. When he saw Farmer Fred bounding toward them, he turned to stand his full height in front of Girl Squirrel to protect her from Farmer Fred.

Farmer Fred paused. Looking at the two squirrels pressed together, he discovered that his heart had changed.

Eating peaches, together with Squirrel, made them even sweeter.

Farmer Fred slowly reached up and picked a peach for himself and another peach for Squirrel. He crouched down to hand Girl Squirrel her half-eaten peach from the ground.

The next day, Farmer Fred began taking down the wall. He invited all the squirrels to share peaches.

The squirrels lounged around on the grass under Tree, their bellies full of peach.

And Farmer Fred and Squirrel's mother wondered whether Squirrel and Girl Squirrel would start a family, so they could have grandsquirrels to love peaches and love Tree.

THE END

Karen Schaufeld is the Co-Founder of All Ages Read Together, an organization dedicated to educating children in need with free preschool programs in their communities. She is also Co-founder and President of 100WomenStrong, which uses strategic philanthropy to improve the lives of local residents. She is an advocate for the growth of renewable energy in Virginia and founded Powered By Facts to spread awareness about Virginia energy policy. Karen resides in Virginia with her husband Fred and has three children and 4 dogs. *How to Eat a Peach* is her third book. She previously published *The Lollipop Tree* and *Larry and Bob*.

Learn More:
www.karenschaufeld.com • www.quidnepress.org
Follow on Facebook

Kurt Schwarz is a realist painter specializing in portraiture, still life, and landscape. His skill in capturing the complex nature of his subjects has contributed to his reputation of being one of Virginia's finest artists. Kurt's career highlights include six solo exhibitions and publication in fine art magazines, including international publication, *The American Artist*.

Learn More:
www.kurtschwarz.com
Follow on Facebook

Fireflies, or lightning bugs, are beetles that are a beautiful symbol of summer. They do not bite and are harmless. Fireflies use chemical bioluminescence or "cold light" to attract a mate. Fireflies are sensitive to land use changes and to artificial light pollution.